CUPID'S ERROR

Joy Avery

CUPID'S ERROR

ISBN-13: 978-1507679593
ISBN-10: 1507679599

First print edition: January 2015

DEDICATION

Dedicated to the dream.

CONTENTS

ACKNOWLEDGMENTS

My thanks—first and foremost—to God for blessing me with this gift of storytelling.

To my husband, Marcus and daughter, Avion—thank you for your unwavering support and patience. I love you both very much!

A huge thank you to Lyla Dune and Jo Ann Mathews. The critiques you two provide are priceless.

To my friends and family who've offered tons and tons of encouragement and support, I express my greatest gratitude.

CHAPTER 1: THE INVITATION

WITH A SHARP TIPPED pen Danica James stabbed at the date printed February 14 on her desk calendar. Crimson-colored ink dirtied the page. She released a grunt. Just like last year, and the year before, and the year before that, she'd be spending Valentine's Day alone.

Who needed high-calorie candy and flowers that would last only a few days? Her head eased against the brown leather chair. She did, that's who. She wanted chocolate. Wanted flowers. Wanted dinner and dancing with a sexy man who had the ability to take her breath away with a simple glance. She wanted the complete Valentine's Day experience.

Releasing a long, drawn out sigh, she lifted her head and snatched up the invitation her best friend placed on the corner of her desk earlier that afternoon.

"Cupid's Arrow Valentine's Day Charity Event."

Danica bit at the corner of her lip. *Hmmm.* It wasn't like she'd be *paying* for a date. Ha. Who was she kidding? That's exactly what she would be doing. Was she really that desperate? It took a beat too long to answer. Maybe she could better respond to the question when she wasn't in the need of some serious sexual healing. Not that she would sleep with some complete stranger on the first date. Well, it couldn't actually be called a date when you're paying for it, right?

She laughed and tossed the thick, red cardstock aside, abandoning the idea of Cupid's Arrow. "Looks like it's going to be me and Mr. Wiggles again this year." She thought about her trusty vibrator. That reminded her, she needed to stock up on batteries.

"Danica?"

Danica glanced up to see her assistant, Lizzy, standing in the doorway. Lizzy twirled a lock of her auburn hair around her finger, something she did when she really didn't want to intrude, but had to. The woman was as timid as a sheltered six-year-old, but worth her weight in gold. No one could organize a hectic schedule like Lizzy.

"What is it, Lizzy?"

Lizzy glanced over her shoulder, then back to Danica. "There's someone—a man—here to see you. He doesn't have an appointment, but is very insistent."

A man enthusiastic to see her? That would be a first. "Did he say what he wanted?"

"No." She tossed another quick glance. Her voice

fell to a whisper. "But I don't think it's business related."

Not business related? If he wasn't there to utilize her services, what could he possibly want? A sinking feeling washed over her, and her instincts kicked into overdrive. The last time a man showed up at her staffing agency—unannounced—he delivered divorce papers.

"What do you want me to tell him?" Lizzy asked in a hushed tone.

With the words cutting into Danica's thoughts, she pushed away from her glass and wood desk, shooing the memory of that dreadful day she'd been served. Coming to a stand, she ironed her hands over her houndstooth pencil skirt, sucked in a deep breath, released it slowly, and said, "Okay. Let's just see what Mr. Mystery wants, shall we?"

Danica stopped dead in her tracks the second her eyes settled on the tuxedo-clad gentleman in front of her. When she'd wished for a tall, dark, handsome man to stroll into her life, she hadn't actually expected it to happen. Maybe next she should wish to hit the lottery.

Handsome held a frosted glass tray with a gold envelope nestled on top of a bed of red roses. The envelope sparkled as if it'd been dipped in glitter. What in the heck was going on?

Gathering her senses, she approached the man. "I'm Danica James. May...I help you?"

The lofty man didn't utter a word as he pushed the tray toward her. Assuming he wanted her to retrieve the envelope, she did. She recognized the emblem pressed into the red wax that sealed the envelope. "Cupid's Arrow?" she asked to no one in particular. She tore into the wrapping.

Dear Ms. James,

On behalf of Cupid's Arrow, I'd like to personally thank you for your generous contribution.

Contribution? "What contribution?" She glanced up at her stone-faced messenger. Yeah, she wasn't going to get any answers out of him, so she continued to read.

Many lives will be touched by your gift. You may not know this, but feeding the hungry has always been a passion of mine. Thanks to you, one less man, woman, or child will go hungry.

I sincerely hope you are looking forward to your Valentine's Day experience with us. It will be an evening you won't soon forget. This, I promise you.

An evening she won't soon forget? Okay. Seriously, what was going on here?

Your Cupid's Fellow will arrive promptly at six o'clock p.m. on Valentine's Day. An evening of fine dining awaits you at the exquisite Avion Shea Steak House. This will be followed by a trip to North Carolina's renowned dessert bar, Chocolate Couture, where you will get the opportunity to custom craft a variety of gourmet items. Afterwards, you'll be whisked to the unrivaled, five-star De Lore Hotel in downtown Raleigh to wrap up the evening with drinks and dancing inside the coveted Horatio Ballroom.

We look forward to making your Valentine's Day one to remember.

Yours sincerely,

Alicia Raven

Danica glanced up from the letter and rubbed the wrinkles that etched themselves in her forehead. "But I didn't—" *Of course.* This had her best friend Savannah's name written all over it. Thanking Handsome, Danica watched the man stroll away. His pristine physique reminded her of just how long it'd been since she'd had an intimate night. *Far, far too long.*

After sending Lizzy to the coffee shop on the corner, Danica returned to her office to call Dead Woman Walking.

"Savannah Washington," danced over the phone line.

"Really? You really bought me a man."

Savannah's laughter poured into the phone. "What are best friends for?"

"To keep each other from doing reckless shit. Like spending an evening with a male gigolo."

"I beg your pardon? Cupid's Arrow is *not* a gigolo service. They are the *elite* in matchmaking, as well as providing distinguished clientele with companions for social events, or whatever the need might be. Anyway, your Valentine's Day experience isn't about either. It's about you not spending another Valentine's Day alone. Plus, it's for a good cause."

Savannah's heart was in the right place, but Danica wasn't sure her mind was. The *minimum* donation for this so-called charity event was five thousand dollars.

Savannah continued. "It's one night, Dani," she said, using the name she dubbed Danica when they met freshman year at North Carolina A&T University. "You won't have to see this man ever again. You're thirty-two years old, but for the past year you've acted more like you're sixty. My grandmother gets more action than you do. Live a little. Be spontaneous. And if he's sexy-as-hell, feel free to take him home and screw his brains out. You have got to have short-circuited Mr. Wiggles by now."

"You are scandalous," Danica said with a chuckle.

Giving it some thought, it actually sounded like a lot of fun. And the De Lore Hotel... She'd wanted to check that place out for forever, but doubted she could even afford a glass of orange juice there, let alone a room. Maybe this wasn't such an atrocious idea after all. She waited for her instincts to shoot off red flags. Nothing. That was a good sign, right? Or maybe the idea was so foolish that her instincts couldn't process it. "Okay, okay. I'll go. You did go through all the trouble. I should at least *appear* grateful."

Savannah squealed over the line. "Yaaay. But you really didn't have a choice. I would have hounded you until you caved."

Danica rested her palm against her forehead. "Do you realize how long it's been since I've gone on a date? Can I even call this a date?"

"It's been far too long, and yes, you can."

"I have absolutely nothing to wear. Especially to a

formal event such as this."

"Say no more. We have two days to hit every store in the 919 area code. You'll have every man in the place wanting to slip you their number, or their tongue."

Danica chortled. *As if*. "But—"

"I don't want to hear any buts. I gotta go. My next client is here. Love you. And we'll talk later."

"But—"

"Kisses."

The line went dead. "Ugh. I hate when she does that."

Danica lowered her head to the desk and moaned. "But what if I make a total ass of myself?"

CHAPTER 2: CUPID'S FELLOW

WESTON HENSHAW TOOK A seat on the edge of his office desk, then crossed his arms over his chest. "I know that look, Alicia. Whatever it is, the answer is no." Which was BS. In all of her twenty-eight years, he couldn't remember the last time he'd said no to his baby sister. Maybe today would be an exception, but he doubted it.

Alicia tossed the folder she'd entered with onto the desk. "Good afternoon to you, too, big brother. Glad to see you're in such a cheerful mood. Surely, we both can't be having a shitty day."

Weston massaged the back of his neck. Yeah, he was being an asshole. But after the phone call he'd just received, it was justified. Not wanting to burden Alicia—who clearly had problems of her own, judging by her uncharacteristic dreariness—he flashed a forced smile. Pushing off the edge of the desk, he moved to his sister and wrapped his arms around her and planted a kiss on the top of her head. "I apologize. It's been a long day. I'm exhausted. What's up?"

Alicia held her arms around him tightly, the way she did when something serious was up. Instantly, he kicked into protective mode.

"You have to quit working so much and live life. It's passing you by," she said.

Not this again. "I'm sure you didn't come here to discuss my work habits."

"You're right." Alicia released a tortured sigh. "I'm in trouble."

Weston held her small frame at arm's length. "You're not pregnant by that—" He stopped himself before he revealed how he truly felt about Alicia's current boyfriend—the sniveling pansy that he was. He detested those rich-boy types. Wouldn't know a day of hard work if it jumped up and bit them in the ass.

Alicia swatted him. "No, I'm not pregnant. I'm smarter than that. Besides, Kevin's a loser. I dumped him two days ago."

Weston tried to hide his delight, but his lips twitched into a smile. "Yes, you are," he said, taking her back into his arms.

"I need your help. You know the Cupid's Arrow Valentine's Day charity event taking place *this* Saturday?"

"Yeah."

"We didn't anticipate just how successful it would be."

9

"That's a good thing, right?"

"It should be, but...there's one *teeny-weeny* little problem."

Why did those words feel like trouble? "Which is?"

"I have more lonely ladies than I have eligible bachelors. I was hoping—"

Weston guided Alicia out of his arms. "Oh, no. Not gonna happen." He saw where this train was headed.

"Please, Bizzy," she said, calling him by the nickname she'd given him when she was younger, because he was always busy with work, or school, or the community. "You know I wouldn't ask unless I really needed your help."

He moved behind his desk and dropped into the chair. "I'm sure there are plenty of other bachelors you can call. Don't you have like a...bachelor reserve, or something?"

"Yes, but they're all spending Valentine's with their significant others."

Significant others? What kind of woman would allow her man to escort other women around town as a profession? He chose not to ask the question aloud. "What makes you think I'm not doing the same?"

Alicia barked a laugh at him. "Really?"

He arched a brow. "Is that so hard to believe?"

She failed miserably at attempting to stifle another laugh. "Okay, I'll play along. One, you don't have a significant other. And two, when was the last time you spent a Valentine's Day away from that desk? If you could, I think you'd marry it."

This desk had been faithful to him for many years, which was more than he could say about the woman in his past. Weston reclined in his chair. "Mocking me is probably not the best way to go about getting something you want. And why should I allow you to pimp me out for the evening, anyway?"

Her eyes brightened as if she'd discovered a new angle of approach. "This could be good for you, Bizzy. Spending an evening with a beautiful woman on your arm. Plus, it's not costing you a dime." She eased into the chair across from him.

This time, it was his opportunity to laugh, because it was his hotel footing the bill. "Not costing me, huh? Do you recall it's De Lore you're utilizing? Full wait staff. Heavy hors d'oeuvres. Open bar. Oh, it's costing me. It's costing me out the ass. And now you want to add me to the menu?" And for the record, he could make one phone call and have a beautiful woman on each arm, but again, chose to keep that to himself.

Alicia slid the folder she'd placed on his desk in front of him. "Please, Bizzy. The client has shelled out big bucks for this. If I have to issue a refund, it's taking food out of the mouths of starving children." Her tone turned sad. "Starving children, Bizzy. Do you really want that?"

Weston chortled. "Now you're going to guilt me?"

"Is it working?"

She knew it was. He sighed heavily for effect. This conversation went like all of their other conversations. She asked. He said no. She said please and batted those big brown doe eyes. He caved. That would probably be the end result this time as well, but he'd draw it out as long as possible. "Okay," he said. "I'll help you out."

Alicia bounced up and down like a child who'd just won a goldfish at the state fair. "Thank you, thank you, thank you, brother. I knew I could count on you."

"Always. You know that." He interlocked his fingers behind his head. "What time does Felipe need to report for duty?"

She frowned as if said goldfish had died on the way home. "Felipe...*your driver*?"

"That's the one. I'm sure he'll jump at the opportunity to spend a lovely evening with a beautiful woman. You need an eligible bachelor. He's your man."

Truth was, Felipe was happily married with kids and would never agree to this, but Alicia didn't know that.

"Your driver is four-foot-one and can barely speak English." Alicia fell back against her chair, closed her eyes and groaned. "Beggars shouldn't be choosers, but..."

Alicia resembled a defeated puppy that'd lost its favorite bone; Weston couldn't bear continuing to torture her. "I'm just kidding. I'll do it." Despite his gut feeling.

She shot forward in the chair, her face as vivid as before. "You will? No joking?"

"Yeah, yeah, yeah. Just send me the details. If this woman turns out to be a psycho, I'm suing."

Alicia bolted from the chair, rounded the desk and

wrapped her arms around Weston's neck tight enough to choke him. "You're the best," she said, planting a kiss on his temple. "I have to go. Big things are happening soon." She scooped up her purse and headed for the door. "Everything you need to know is in that red folder. Likes, dislikes. You have to make this woman feel like she's soaring." She winked at him. "You'll do fine."

Something occurred to him. "This better not be another one of your attempts at marrying me off."

"Not this time, I promise. And for once, could you please eat an actual meal and not pig-out on appetizers? Show this woman you're a modern man, not a caveman."

"You know I don't go for all of those fancy-schmancy meals. I like potato skins, nachos, southwestern eggrolls." His stomach growled, and he glanced at his watch. He could really go for a good burger.

"And that's okay...when you're at *Chili's*. This is Avion Shea. *The* Avion Shea."

Regardless of what he ordered, like always, he'd be the only one enjoying the meal. Seemed as if every woman he went out with was on a diet of some sort. He could always predict her meal. Green salad and water.

Alicia started again. "And for goodness sakes, keep it in your pants."

"Really, Alicia? You're as bad as that ridiculous magazine article last year. I'm thirty-four years old. I am plenty capable of not screwing everything in a skirt."

"I know you are, big brother. I'm only giving you a

hard time. You're the most honorable man I know. Any woman would be lucky to have you. I love you." She blew him a kiss before escaping through the door.

Weston laughed as the door clicked shut. Clearly, Alicia knew what the outcome would be. She'd already prepared the dossier. He shook his head and opened the folder. "Not bad," he said, staring down at the beauty. "Not bad at all."

CHAPTER 3: THAT SEXY RED DRESS

WESTON POUNDED AN OPEN hand against his oak desk with enough force to rattle the pens in the brown leather holder, then shook his hand to alleviate the sting. With the desk phone pressed to his ear, he paced back and forth. The conversation with his lawyer wasn't going as smoothly as he'd liked. Why hadn't he followed his first instinct and ignored the man's email until after his Cupid's Arrow obligation?

"That's bullshit, Ralph. What the hell am I paying your firm for? Surely not for you to tell me you think we should settle out of court."

"Just listen, Weston—"

"No, you listen. Settling would suggest guilt. I haven't done anything wrong."

If Weston had to guess, Ralph sat behind his desk, eyes closed, massaging his temples. He'd represented The Henshaw Group for over ten years and knew when

Weston was this passionate about something, there was no talking him down. De Lore was Weston's baby. And he'd be damned if he allowed someone's get-rich-quick scheme to tarnish the hotel's impeccable reputation, or his.

In a steady tone, Ralph said, "He's not suing you, Weston. He's suing De Lore."

Weston's tone rose an octave higher than he'd intended. "I am De Lore. An attack against my hotel is an attack against me personally. Wrongful termination? The asshole was a damn pervert who harassed my female staff. There's zero tolerance for that kind of behavior at De Lore, or any of my companies for that matter. Furthermore—" He caught a glimpse of the clock. *Shit*. "Look, Ralph, I didn't mean to bite your head off. I know I'm in good hands. We'll have to continue this discussion later. There's someplace I need to be."

Weston heard the relief in Ralph's voice when he spoke. He hated he'd gotten so riled up, but he despised swindlers. He'd dealt with too many throughout the years. Men who thought they could get one over on him because of his young age.

"Okay, bud. We'll talk soon," Ralph said. "No settling."

"No settling."

Ending the call, Weston snatched his tuxedo coat and overcoat off the back of his chair and darted for the exit. Two minutes later, he cruised down a lively Fayetteville Street. Women and men wore red in celebration of Valentine's Day. Again, he questioned himself how he'd let Alicia talk him into this. Too late to back out now.

He glanced at his watch, recalling his sister's warning from earlier. *Don't. Be. Late*. The words rang in his ears like church bells. She'd strangle him if she knew he was going to be just that...late.

Something told him not to swing by the office for "just a minute." *Wrongful termination? The bastard was lucky I didn't chop off the body part he flashed at my laundry crew*. He shook his head, scrambling the thoughts of his looming legal battle.

Weston bent forward. "Hey, buddy, you think you could speed this pony up a bit?" The driver had to be going ten miles under the speed limit. Weston had watched a little girl on a tricycle peddle past them.

Weston needed Felipe behind the wheel. There would be no worries about getting there on time. The twenty minute drive would have taken only ten. Twelve at the most. The man drove like a blind bat out of hell. He had the speeding tickets and outrageous insurance premiums to prove it. But Felipe always got him where he needed to be, in one piece and on time.

"Yes, sir," the young man said, giving the vehicle more gas.

That's more like it.

Weston rested his head against the back of the seat and gazed out the window. As much as he hated to admit it, Alicia was right. He needed a life. Or more out of the one he already had. Maybe it was time. Time to stop putting so much emphasis on work. Time to rejoin the living world. Time to focus on his love life—or lack of one.

"So, did my sister give you strict instructions to report my every move tonight?" he asked the limo driver, never taking his eyes off the passing world outside the window.

"No, sir."

"Right."

This was not how he'd intended to spend Valentine's Day. With a woman he'd never met before. And with his luck, she would turn out to be a complete wacko. Hopefully Alicia vetted her female clientele as thoroughly as she did her male.

Weston glanced at his watch again when they finally pulled curbside in front of a two-story brick home in a cozy neighborhood off Falls of the Neuse Road.

Fifteen minutes late. *Damn*. He hoped she—Grace, the profile stated—wasn't a stickler for time. Without waiting for his driver to open the door, he bolted from the vehicle the second they came to a complete stop.

Even though it was February, the grass was as green as if it were the middle of summer. That was one thing he missed, having a yard. He definitely couldn't see the grass from his place. He rang the bell and waited. No answer. Maybe Grace did have a thing about punctuality. He adjusted his black, double-breasted overcoat and jabbed at the buzzer again. He thought he heard movement. Finally, the door crept open.

Weston's lips parted slightly, but no words escaped. Never had he been stunned speechless...until now. The red evening gown hugged her curves as if the dress had been painted on by a master artist. A plunging neckline revealed a tasteful amount of cleavage, while the thigh-high split revealed a gorgeous, honey-toned leg that went on for forever.

His crotch grew tight. Under different circumstances, he'd have already planned the best strategy for removing the delicate fabric, because the night would have ended in hot, sweaty sex. But this was different. This was business. His sister's business. And if he screwed with it—no pun intended—she'd kill him. And he wouldn't do anything to jeopardize the reputation she'd worked so hard to obtain.

Her dark brown hair was pulled into a neat, tight bun on top of her head, drawing attention to a neck crafted for warm kisses. This woman exuded the perfect amount of sexiness. She also caused him to imagine doing deliciously naughty things to her.

And her scent. Vanilla? Jesus. She smelled like a batch of fresh baked sugar cookies. His favorite. He could eat an entire tray of them. His brain banished the wicked thoughts materializing.

Weston's body didn't forfeit the opportunity to remind him that he was all man. He fought down the swell in his boxers, reminding himself why he was there. But who could blame him for his potent attraction to her? A goddess in red.

There was just one question. Had Cupid's made an error? This was *not* the woman in the dossier he'd been given.

♡♡♡

Danica stood in the foyer and eyed the door as if it would explode. The phrase *do or die* raced through her head. Her Cupid's Fellow had already rung the bell twice, but her feet rooted to the spot where she stood.

"You're being ridiculous, Danica. You can do this. It's not like it's even a real date. This is someone who has been paid to show you a good time," she mumbled. The words uprooted her feet. "A few boring hours. How difficult could it be?"

The three-inch shimmery gold stilettos she wore clanked across the tiled floor. Her hand rested on the handle, anticipation building. All day she'd imagined how her Cupid's Fellow would look, coming to the conclusion he'd more than likely be easy on the eyes, but nothing to write home about. That was okay. Average, she could handle. Arrogant, not so much so.

Taking a deep breath, she eased the door open.
Oh.

She'd never experienced a wrinkle in time, but imagined it had to be similar to this. Everything around her came to a standstill, including her ability to speak.

She'd seen her fair share of handsome men, but this one here...called to her. His skin was the same hue of the whipped chocolate frosting her grandmother used to spread over Danica's favorite butter cake. A warm sensation crawled through her, sending her body into a sexual tizzy. Damn, she craved a piece of that cake now. She may have even glided her tongue across her bottom lip, as if tasting him—it—the cake.

Every exquisite inch of him tantalized her. Those piercing brown eyes and strong jawline commanded attention. And she was more than happy to oblige. Beards had never been her thing, but he wore his well— precisely trimmed and not too thick.

Whipped Chocolate flashed a look of confusion. If she had to guess, he was gauging her sanity. Understandable, since she eyed him like prey.

"I apologize for keeping you waiting," she finally spat out.

A brilliant smile spread across his face, banishing his quizzical expression. "I was beginning to think you'd stood me up."

"Well, it would have been justified. You are fifteen minutes late." She smiled a moment later. "I'm just giving you a hard time."

He chuckled. "Guilty. But I promise I'll make it up to you."

Even the man's chuckle dizzied her. *You already have*. Savannah's words played in her head. *If he's sexy-as-hell, take him home and screw his brains out*. That wasn't such a bad idea. Not a bad idea at all.

With her next breath, Danica performed a mental forehead slap. What in the hell was she saying? It was a bad idea. She didn't know this man from Adam. Plus, she didn't do one-night stands. The first and last one she'd had, she'd ended up marrying the lowlife. Besides, she scanned the lofty man, something told her one night with him would not be enough.

"Danica James," she said, jabbing her hand toward him. The second he captured it, the sensation came close to buckling her knees.

His furrowed brows smoothed. "Pardon my manners. Weston Henshaw. It's a pleasure to meet you, *Danica.*"

He said her name as if she'd given him an alias. Strange.

"Have we met before?" Danica asked. Something about him was vaguely familiar. Or was she simply confusing him with one of the male models she'd seen in a catalogue? With the way he carried himself, model was possible.

"I'm sure I would remember meeting you," he said.

The way he eyed her with appreciation, she was glad she'd let Savannah talk her into buying the overpriced dress. Weston flashed another heart-stopping smile, drawing her attention to his luscious lips. *Mmm.*

The lingering grip he held on her hand finally loosened and his arm swept toward a black, stretch limo. "Shall we?" he asked.

Wow. Cupid's Arrow really knew how to do it up. "Yes. I just need to grab my coat."

After he'd helped her into the ankle-length red wool coat, they moved toward the luxury vehicle. Danica could feel his eyes on her. When she rotated her head to face him, he flashed a half-smile and glanced away. She refused to believe he was shy.

Weston dismissed the driver, opting to open the door for her himself. *Well played.* As he rounded the car, Danica couldn't shake the feeling that she knew him from somewhere. Had he used her agency in the past? No. There was no way she would have forgotten him.

The temperature inside the car was in stark contrast to the icy forty degrees outside. As the old folks would say, it felt like snow. The idea of a snowfall delighted her. The notion of making snow cream, even more.

"You seem nervous," Weston said, settling in dangerously close to her.

"Nervous? No." She chuckled. "Okay, maybe a little."

"Why?"

"Why?" Jesus. She sounded like a parrot. "It's been a long time since I've done...this."

"Done what? Gone on a date?" he asked nonchalantly.

"Is that what we're calling this?" Danica shifted toward him slightly, causing the slit of her dress to reveal more thigh than she'd intended. Weston didn't seem to mind, as his eyes raked over the exposed flesh.

When she cleared her throat, his gaze rose. This was going to be an interesting evening. Especially if he continued to gaze at her with those bedroom eyes.

Weston made no apologizes for his ogling. "Isn't that what this is? A man. A woman. Dinner, dessert, dancing."

"A date would suggest we met under normal circumstances. You asked me out; I accepted. That's not exactly what happened here."

Weston captured her hand and kissed the back. "Ms. James, may I have the honor of spending the evening with you? A date, if we're labeling it."

Danica smirked, feeling unusually comfortable with Weston. "You've got this Cupid's Fellow thing down pat, don't you?" All of that charm could be dangerous. The way his eyes searched her face, unnerved her.

"You look amazing, Danica James."

"Thank you. You're quite dapper yourself, Weston Henshaw."

Then he smiled, relaxed against the seat, and shifted his focus out the window. Danica's eyes lowered to their still joined hands. Cupid's Arrow trained their men well. But she couldn't forget that this was all a part of the fantasy, the Valentine's experience. After this evening, she would become a figment of his imagination.

CHAPTER 4: CHOCOLATE TEMPTATION

WESTON COULDN'T EXPLAIN WHAT was going on with him. He'd claimed Danica's hand in the limo, now he couldn't take his eyes off her at the dinner table. Every time her lips wrapped around the fork, he tingled below the belt. God, he wanted to taste her mouth, smear that seductive red lipstick all over her face.

"You've barely touched your plate," Danica said, drawing Weston's attention.

"I enjoy watching you. You're not shy about food. I like that."

She placed her fork down and dabbed at the corners of her mouth. "I was so ner—"

He chuckled when Danica banished her thought, but had a good idea *nervous* was the word she'd abandoned. If she was nervous now, he couldn't tell.

"I skipped lunch today. I had to make sure I could

get into this dress."

"I'm glad you did. I would have hated being denied the opportunity to experience you in that dress. And, apparently, I'm not the only one."

Weston took the opportunity to survey the room. The second they'd entered Avion Shea, Danica became the focus of nearly every man present. She hadn't seemed interested in the attention, but the idea that they were undressing her with their eyes tightened his jaw. The fact that he'd had any reaction was ridiculous. Danica wasn't his woman.

Danica didn't shift her eyes away from him to acknowledge her would-be suitors. "But you're the only one who matters, right? I'm here with you."

Ahh. He wasn't the only one in a flirtatious mood. "Careful. You might swell my head." *Again*, but he kept that part to himself.

Her eyes slid to his plate. "Let me guess, you're a fruits and veggies man."

"What makes you say that?"

"You've hardly touched your steak or potatoes."

He flashed a half-smile. "I had salt and vinegar chips for breakfast today, and a honey bun and chocolate milk for lunch."

"Huh. You're a junk-foodie, too. You must work out quite a bit." Her eyes slid to his arms. "You're in *great* shape."

He lifted his glass of wine to his lips. "You checking me out, Danica James?" Then took a sip of the sweet white wine.

"I'm merely making an observation."

A brief silence fell between them as they stared across the table at one another. He fought the image of her lying beneath him, moaning his name. "So, what do you like to do when you're not painting the town red?" Weston asked. "Get it? Painting the town red." His eyes trailed to her dress.

"Clever," she said with a laugh. "I watch the History Channel. *Ax Men, Swamp People, Ice Road Truckers*. Go ahead and laugh."

"Are you kidding me? *Swamp People* and *Ice Road Truckers* are my shows. I don't miss an episode." Weston relaxed in his seat, lifting his glass again. "I guess we have a few things in common."

"I guess we do," Danica said, a faint smile touching her lips. "So, Weston, how long have you been with Cupid's Arrow?"

He released an inward groan. He'd hoped she wouldn't ask that question. Not lying, but not fully telling the truth either, he said, "I've been associated with the company for a number of years." Which was more truth than deception. He was a silent partner at his sister's company. Very silent.

"I'm sure you're requested often. You're quite the charmer."

"Not as often as you might think." It was his turn to query her relationship with Cupid's. "Is this your first time using their services?" He couldn't imagine her not being able to get a companion on her own.

"Yes. And I wasn't actually given much of a

choice."

Weston's brows creased. "What does that mean?"

Danica laughed and eyed the vaulted ceiling. "I can't believe I'm about to tell you this." Bringing her attention back to him, she said, "My best friend gifted you to me."

"Gifted me, huh?"

Her expression turned stern. "Wow. That sounded so degrading. I apologize. I didn't mean to insult you. I respect what you do. You make lonely women feel...not so lonely."

Weston held up his hand. "No offense taken." Their gazes held while silence fell between them. Pushing his plate away, he leaned forward and clasped his hands together on the table. "Is that what you are? Lonely?"

"Sometimes," she said without hesitation.

Sadness shadowed her otherwise jovial manner. It bothered him that he'd been the one to cause it with his inquiry. "Not tonight," he said, then relaxed in his seat again. "You won't be lonely tonight." And he meant every word of it.

♡♡♡

If Danica had known Chocolate Couture would be this delicious, she'd have suggested they skip dinner and came straight for dessert. The smooth chocolate melted on her tongue and caused a celebration in her mouth.

"*Oh. My. God, Becky*," Danica said. "This is the best chocolate I've ever put into my mouth, and I've had a lot of chocolate in my mouth." She groaned inwardly. Had she really just said that out loud? More urgently, had those words sounded as sexual to Weston as they had to her?

Weston laughed, picking up another piece of the delectable treats. "Who's Becky?"

"Sir Mix-a-Lot?"

Weston arched a questioning brow.

"Baby Got Back? Come on, I know you've heard the song."

Awareness seemed to set in. "Ah, got it."

"I picked it up from Savannah. My best friend," she added.

"I hope you know that song is going to be stuck in my head all night." He positioned the candy inches from her lips. "Open up."

Without giving it a second's worth of thought, she complied. She'd only known Weston roughly four hours, but it felt as if she'd known him all of her life. The notion rattled her. It'd never crossed her mind that she would enjoy herself this much with a complete stranger. Plus, they had things in common. But a love for junk food and the History Channel hardly qualified them as soul mates. Not that she was looking for love, she reminded herself.

Weston's fingers grazed her lips as he slid the treat into her mouth. She moaned from the warm sensation that traveled down her torso and settled between her legs. A one-night-stand was beginning to look quite enticing.

"I was going to ask if that one got an '*Oh, my God, Becky*', too, but I think I like that moan much better," he said.

Feeling a bit embarrassed, she stammered out, "Y-You're good at mixing flavors." Good at a lot more, too, she would bet. "Cointreau and Grand Marnier. Who would have thought?"

Weston popped the remainder of the orange flavored chocolate into his mouth. "Mmm, that is good. Maybe I should invest in a chocolate shop. What do you think?"

Watching him suck the remnants of melted chocolate from the tip of his finger snatched Danica's focus. Snapping out of her trance, she said, "Something tells me whatever you put your mind to will become a success. But then, what would Cupid's Arrow do without you?" She smirked and strolled away. "This place is amazing. I never even knew it existed."

Three crystal chandeliers hung from the high ceilings of the converted warehouse. The entire space was decorated in shades of purple. And the smell... Intoxicating. She'd never seen so much chocolate in one place in her life. A sign read: A CHOCOLATE LOVER'S PARADISE. She agreed.

Danica's eyes widened. "Is that a stiletto made out of chocolate?" Shoes and chocolate, two of her favorite things. But a shoe made of chocolate...priceless.

"Check this out," Weston said from behind her.

When she joined him, her jaw dropped. A train, at least three feet high and sculpted completely out of chocolate was on display, encased in glass. The engine, box cars, and the caboose were all intricately crafted.

"Can you imagine the time it took to do this?" Weston said.

He seemed absolutely fascinated by the display. While his focus lingered on the work of art, hers lingered on him—a finely crafted piece of chocolate, as well. Even though she was wearing heels, he stood about four inches taller than she. Six-three, if she had to guess. Well-toned, from what she could see. Where was a genie when she needed one? Her first wish...x-ray vision. For now, she'd just have to leave it to her imagination.

Weston spoke, yanking her back to reality.

"My dad and I used to build trains together." He touched the glass as if he were remembering a special moment. A beat later, he yanked his hand away as if he realized what he was doing. "You ready?" he asked, shifting toward her.

Whatever memories he relived hit him hard, altering his entire demeanor. The light that'd shined in him dimmed. In his eyes, she witnessed sadness and pain. "Sure," she said. As they sauntered toward the exit in silence, she touched Weston's arm. "Are you okay?"

"Yeah." He ran a hand over his head. "Yeah, I'm good."

"You're disappointed that you couldn't break that

glass and devour all of that chocolate?"

He laughed and the old Weston returned. "Name something that means the world to you," he said.

Danica found the question totally random, but answered anyway. "My office desk."

Weston eyed her. "Your office desk?"

She nodded. "It was given to me by someone special."

"Ah. Okay." He shifted his focus straight ahead.

For some reason, Danica desperately wanted him to inquire about her "someone special." Maybe that would mean he was interested. She chastised herself. *This is only one-night. Tomorrow, you return to the same old lonely Danica. Don't get caught up.*

"An ex?" Weston asked casually.

A smile curved her lips. "My mother."

"Your mother?"

"Yes. She'd been encouraging me to start my own business, but it never felt like the right time. I'd gone through a nasty divorce. I was strapped for funds. I was in a not-so-good place in my life—" Jesus. Why was she telling this man all of her business? Sometimes her mouth moved quicker than her brain. Luckily, he didn't query her on anything she'd just said.

"What happened to change your mind about starting your own business?"

She eyed him a second or two before continuing. "I was on my mother's sofa thumbing through a furniture catalogue, just passing time. I came across the most gorgeous wooden and glass desk I'd ever seen. It was *ridiculously* expensive. Something like six thousand dollars. Jokingly, I told my mother if I had that desk, I'd start my business that day." She stared straight ahead. "Two weeks later, it was delivered to my front door." She shook her head, recalling the moment.

Weston pushed open the door for her to exit. "Wow."

Danica batted her eyes as tears welled in them. "There was absolutely no way my mother could afford that desk. I finally wrangled out of her how she did."

"How did she afford it?"

Danica liked the fact that Weston seemed genuinely interested in her story. Talking to him was so easy. "She'd withdrawn the money from her retirement fund." A tear slid down her face. She stopped. "I'm sorry. I cry every time I recall it. You must think I'm insane," she said, lifting her hand to swipe the tear away. Weston captured her hand before she could.

"I think you're sentimental. That's a great quality. Your mother sounds like a wonderful woman." He glided his thumb across her cheek.

Something happened in that moment, and by the way he stared into her eyes, he felt it too. Her eyes slid to his mouth, then away with urgency before she did exactly what she wanted to do, kiss him. "She is," she said absently.

Weston's hand rested on the side of her neck a second before gliding it to the back and pulling her mouth slowly to his. The anticipation awakened every inch of her body. Her nipples hardened when he inched his free hand down her ribcage. She wanted this. More than she'd wanted anything in a very long time.

With his lips inches from hers, he said, "I'm sure this is breaking protocol, but some rules are meant to be broken. I'll suffer the consequences."

No, no, no. Why did he have to go and say that? With their mouths so close that she could feel his heat escape, she pulled away. She wouldn't be the reason why he lost his job.

Not only that, what would happen after the kiss? He surely wouldn't resign a position he'd held for years. Not for a woman he'd only known one night. And she certainly wouldn't be okay with his job—escorting lonely women about town.

Why did any of that matter anyway? It wasn't like he was asking her to be his. *Slow it down, Danica. You're getting too far ahead of yourself.* The more she thought about it, maybe this was simply another part of the Valentine's experience. Either way, kissing him was a lose-lose situation. All she had to do was keep reminding herself of that.

CHAPTER 5: THIS CHANGES EVERYTHING

DANICA'S REJECTION OUTSIDE OF Chocolate Couture only made Weston want her more. How could he come so close to what he'd fantasized about since he'd first laid eyes on her, and blow it sky-high? Damn. He should have done less talking and more doing.

The streetlights whizzed by, making the world outside the limo's window resemble a colorful blur. Another two hours and their fantasy evening would be over. He dreaded midnight.

How could he be this wrapped up? Especially in a woman he'd only known a few hours. What in the hell was happening to him? His attraction to Danica wasn't all about sex. Sure, he'd fantasized about how good it would feel to drive himself deep inside of her, but even without the prospect of sex, he enjoyed being with her. They clicked.

Danica's soft tone tore into his thoughts.

"Are you upset?"

Weston faced her, her tender eyes apologetic. He wanted to tell her everything. How he wasn't an employee of Cupid's. How it felt like he'd known her all of his life. How he wanted her like no other woman before. "Of course not. You saved me from myself. I should apologize to you. I was out of line."

"Don't apologize," she said, shifting her focus back out the window.

Had she wanted him to kiss her? If so, why'd she push him away? He'd allowed her lips to slip away once, it wouldn't happen again.

Twenty minutes later, they pulled in front of the De Lore Hotel. He'd instructed his employees not to acknowledge him. Another stipulation placed on him by Alicia. This entire evening was shrouded in secrets. It was draining.

"I've admired this place for years," Danica said. "I did a virtual tour when it first opened. My jaw dropped."

"You've never visited De Lore?"

"Are you kidding? I couldn't afford a bottle of water in this place. I hear there's a penthouse that spans four levels."

"Three," he said. "Or so I've heard."

When they entered the elevator, the attendant's face glowed. "Mr. Hen—" He stalled as if remembering Weston's instruction. "I mean… Sir… Ah…" Chester glanced away. "What floor?"

"Twenty-four," Weston said.

The elevator started a smooth ascent. The only sound in the cabin was that of the turning gears. Danica would've had to be oblivious not to have picked up on Chester's odd behavior.

When they slowed to a stop, Chester announced, "Twenty-fourth floor." He never made eye contact when he added, "You folks enjoy your evening."

Inside the hallway, Danica faced Weston. "Do you know him?"

He glanced back for effect. "I...don't think so."

"He seemed to know you."

"Yeah, he did. That was strange. Maybe I have one of those faces. You thought you knew me, remember?"

The look on her face told him she was skeptical of his response, but she didn't press the issue. They ambled down the extended hall, coming up on two tuxedo-clad men standing guard outside the oversized doors of the Horatio Ballroom.

The ballroom was named after his father, a man who defined the meaning of hard work. A man he missed dearly. On their approach, the men opened the doors, and he and Danica were transported into another dimension. One steeped in red and gold.

"Whoa," Danica said, taking in every inch of the room.

Even he was in awe of the transformation. Alicia had done her thing with the room. He'd never seen it look so amazing. The red and gold theme complimented the ivory-colored marble throughout the room. Dozens of tall glass vases that glowed at the base held what appeared to be thousands of red roses.

Several food stations were scattered around the room. Men and women dressed in black and white carried frosted glass trays holding flutes of champagne. A ten-person band rocked the stage, singing Otis Redding's "Cupid." He was thoroughly impressed. And that wasn't easy to do.

After Weston checked their coats, Danica grabbed his hand and pulled him with her. "Let's dance."

She didn't give him the opportunity to object as she ushered him toward the large crowd gathered on the dance floor. Not that he would have passed up an opportunity to get close to her anyway.

He spotted his sister mingling with guests. When she mouthed the word "Wow," he agreed with a knowing smile.

As fate would have it, one of the female singers took to the mic and crooned Minnie Riperton's "Inside My Love." The suggestive song seemed to be directed at them. *Two people, just meeting* described them. *Barely touching each other...* Now that was a stretch because they were definitely touching.

Danica hadn't been shy about walking into his arms. Heat raged inside of him as he held her snug against his chest. His hand slowly glided along the soft fabric of her dress and rested on the small of her back. He could be wrong, but he swore she trembled.

Danica hummed softly as they moved with an unhurried rhythm, clinging to one another like two perfectly suited gloves. His body reacted in the way any red-blooded man's body would react when there was a beautiful woman pressed so tightly against him.

"I love this song," she said.

The words pulled Weston from his fantasy of making love to her. "They say this song isn't about sex, but it sounds pretty sexual to me."

Danica pulled back and glanced up at him. "I don't know. I kind of agree with Ms. Riperton. She said this song is about something far deeper than just sex."

A beat later the woman with the mic belted out, "Do you want to ride inside my love?"

Danica laughed. "But the lyrics are pretty risqué."

The song ended, and the tempo increased. They danced to song after song. After close to an hour of moving and shaking, Danica finally tired. He would have gone on for hours, if it meant being close to her.

"I think I need a break," she said. "My feet are protesting."

He led her to an empty two-top table draped in a shiny red satiny fabric and sprinkled with white rose petals. Gold votive candles flickered, making the quaint table feel romantic. Once he'd pulled out Danica's chair and she'd lowered into it, he occupied the one across from her.

She glanced toward the stage. "This band is amazing. Are they local?"

"I don't know, but I'm sure I can find out for you. You like to dance, I see."

"Love to dance, actually. Just haven't in a while."

"There seems to be a lot of things you haven't done in a while." That familiar sadness returned to her face. *Idiot*. Before he could correct his rash words, over Danica's shoulder, he spotted his sister motioning for him. And she didn't look pleased.

♡♡♡

Danica decided to explore the room while Weston talked to a young, attractive woman, mid-twenties, if she had to guess. A tinge of— *Nope*. She refused to call it jealousy. She hadn't known him long enough to be jealous. And she wasn't territorial.

"You shouldn't be standing here alone. Especially in that dress."

She rotated to face the baritone voice behind her. Mocha-toned and handsome. Not Weston Henshaw handsome, but not everyone could be so fortunate.

"May I buy you a drink...?"

With extended hand, she said, "Danica." She chose to keep her last name to herself. He wrapped his large hand around hers. *Soft*. Entirely too soft for a man's hand.

"Danica. A beautiful name for a beautiful woman."

When he made circles on the back of her hand with his thumb, she pulled away. Something about this man made her uneasy. Being polite, she asked, "And you are?"

"*Calvin Fairchild*."

Danica glanced over her shoulder, her gaze

slamming into a stone-faced Weston. He didn't appear none-too-happy to see the man occupying her time. Was Calvin Fairchild competition?

"Weston Henshaw. I'm surprised to see you here," Calvin said.

"Well, you never know when I'll pop up. You should know that." He rested his hands on Danica's waist. "Good seeing you, Calvin." They moved away.

Why was Weston acting like an overprotective lover? It flattered and confused her. More flattered. It'd been a long time since a man had shown her so much attention. Unfortunately, she had a feeling Weston's reaction stemmed from more personal reasons and less about her.

"Did the guy sleep with your girlfriend or something?"

"My fiancée, actually."

Shit. Talk about putting your foot in your mouth. "I'm sorry, Weston. I didn't—"

"How could you have known?" he said, finishing her thought.

Danica suspected Calvin's approach hadn't been a coincidence. Had he done it to get under Weston's skin? Of course he had. And he'd pulled her into the mix. *Bastard*.

She took Weston's hand and led him back to the dance floor.

"I thought your feet hurt," he said.

"Just follow my lead."

On the dance floor, she nonchalantly searched the

room for Calvin. Sure his eyes were pinned to them, she made Weston the object of her affection. More like obsession, the way her body gyrated sensually, sexually against his.

She hadn't expected to make Weston moan, but she had. The sound gave her even more courage. Assuring they hadn't lost the attention of the bastard, she took things a step further. "Kiss me."

Weston's facial expression flashed stunned and his active motion stilled. "What did you say?"

"He's watching. Kiss me. It's okay." She intertwined her fingers behind his head and inched his mouth closer.

The anticipation lit every fuse in her body. Why couldn't second thoughts happen first?

♡♡♡

"Who's looking?" Weston asked, his mouth so close to Danica's that her warm breath tickled his nose.

"The bastard. *Calvin*," she said as if he should have known. "Now kiss me."

The idea of Danica seeking revenge on his behalf made him smile. This woman was something else. And that something else drew him closer to her flame. But despite how much he wanted to kiss her, could he really allow her to put herself out there like this? Especially over the bastard, as she'd labeled him.

"Weston Henshaw, are you afraid to kiss me in public?"

He smirked. She clearly hadn't known him long enough. "Are you sure about this?"

Searching his eyes, she said, "Make it count."

Make it count? Not only would he make it count, he'd make her rattle in those sexy ass gold shoes. He wrapped his arms around her waist and held her flush against his chest. He'd dreamt about kissing her all night long and would be damned if the opportunity slipped away again.

Make it count. Hell, he'd make her walls wobble.

"Just remember," he said, "you asked for this."

He lowered his mouth to hers, giving a gentle peck. No sense rushing it. Ignoring the fact a hundred people surrounded them, he parted her lips with his tongue. Her mouth—warm and soft—scrambled his brain. What started off slow and controlled soon turned needful and unruly. A hunger he couldn't manage caused him to ravish Danica's mouth.

She tasted delicious. Sweet like fine chocolate. The swell in his pants should have given him the strength he needed to pull away before he took them both up in flames. No such luck.

His body continued to defy him. The pounding in his boxers. The beading of his nipples. The tightening deep in his gut. And then there were Danica's moans— soft and continuous—that amplified every pleasurable effect vice-gripping his body.

"You never kiss me like that, Thomas, and we've been married twenty years."

The elegant voice came from his left. A beat later,

Danica pulled away. His jaw tightened, and he cursed the elderly couple next to them for snatching him away from paradise.

Danica stared up at him wide-eyed and agape. Something gentle danced in her eyes. Oh yeah, he'd made it count. "Maybe we should sit," he said when she seemed unsteady on her feet.

Catching a glimpse of Calvin, he spotted the scowl from across the room. Revenge served hot or cold had never been Weston's thing, but it would be a lie to say the man's displeasure hadn't given him a twinge of satisfaction.

Settling at the table, he reached down and captured Danica's foot. "Here, let me see if I can help your aching feet. I know they have to be killing you now."

"What are you—?"

Before she could finish her thought, he had her shoe off and began kneading her beautiful foot. He'd never considered himself a foot man, but for this foot, he could make an exception. It felt like cotton in his hand. The glittery polish sparkled every time light hit her toes.

"—doing?" Her eyes closed and her head tilted back slowly. "Oh, God. That...feels...amazing. I may have to keep you."

I'm all yours. He didn't dare let the words slip passed his lips. "Thank you for what you did out there."

Her head came up. "It felt good to finally be on the winning end." Her gaze settled on him for a moment.

"My ex-husband had an affair—*numerous* affairs," she corrected. "It... I can relate to what you went through."

Weston didn't reveal to Danica that Calvin had actually done him a favor. Once he'd ended things, Weston came to the realization his ex hadn't been the woman for him. He'd stayed with her out of habit. He didn't like change. Looking back, he wasn't sure how he'd tolerated her frigid, unaffectionate manner for two years. Why he'd ever proposed in the first place still puzzled him.

"Do you still love her?" Danica asked.

The question slammed him back to reality. "No." His turn. "Do you still love your ex-husband?"

"God, no. Loathe, yes. Love, no. Hell, no."

Weston chuckled. "Okay, tell me how you really feel."

"I really like you."

Danica's body stiffened. She eyed him in the way one did when they regretted saying something they hadn't intended to say. At least, intended to say out loud. He chuckled at the expression on her face—a mix of shock and regret.

"I really like you, too," he said.

A slow smile curled her lips.

"Your smile could light a room."

"I bet you say that to all the girls."

He winked at her. This woman held no punches.

"Can I ask you something, Weston?"

He shrugged. "Shoot."

"I know we don't know each other all that well...

And it's okay to tell me it's none of my business."

This sounded serious. "Okay," he said, never breaking eye contact with her.

"At Chocolate Couture. The train display. I recognized the pain in your eyes. What happened?"

Weston lowered his head and focused on her foot. He didn't like remembering the accident. Staring at the train tonight had forced him to.

Danica rested her warm hand on the side of his face. "I'm sorry. I shouldn't have asked. Sometimes I'm too inquisitive for my own good."

He brought his gaze back to hers, rubbing his rough cheek against her hand. The tenderness in her eyes softened the ache in his chest. "My sixteenth birthday, my father got me this amazing train set. We worked six hours straight assembling that sucker." He paused a moment, reliving the scene in his head. "When we got ready to fire it up, my dad realized he'd forgotten the batteries." He glanced away briefly. "It was late. Ten o'clock or better. But my dad was determined that I would get to fire it up on my birthday. He headed to the nearby store." Weston swallowed hard and lowered his eyes again. "He never made it. A drunk—" His voice cracked and he paused to clear his throat.

Danica reclaimed her foot, bolted from her seat, ushered him to his feet and wrapped her loving arms around him. He reciprocated. They held tightly to one another for what felt like an eternity, her gentle hand moving up and down his back.

A phrase his mother used to say popped into his head. *Sometimes all we need is a hug.* A hug had worked back then, and it worked now. And for the first time since he could remember, reliving his father's death didn't paralyze him.

Once she'd freed him from her arms, she rested her hands on his chest. "Are you okay?"

He nodded. "Yeah, I'm good."

She studied him as if attempting to ascertain the validity of his response. Her eyes finally slid away.

"Is that a photo booth?" Danica asked.

A photo booth? Weston glanced over his shoulder. "Looks like it."

She donned a wide grin. "Let's take a picture."

The suggestion gave him the out he needed. Another second and he would have captured that beautiful mouth of hers again. He'd have made that time count, too.

Trailing her across the floor, the sway of her deliciously curved hips rebooted his hunger for her. What was it about Danica? How could he be addicted to her and hadn't even experienced his first hit, so to speak?

"Oh," she said, after pulling back the red draping and peeping inside the black structure. "It's quite...cozy."

Intimate. He seized this opportunity. "We can make it work." He stepped inside and claimed a seat on the tiny bench. When he reached for her hand, protest danced across her face. Luckily, it only lasted a moment.

A half a second after she settled into his lap, he regretted extending the invitation. Her warmth and sweet scent aroused a need that threatened to consume him.

"Do you know how to work this thing," she asked, shifting in his lap.

He groaned at the friction. "Maybe we should—"

"Ah. Here we go."

She pressed a green button. Seconds later, the screen blazed navy blue. Oversized white numbers counted down from thirty with an annoying *bloop* each time a second peeled away.

Weston wanted to place kisses to the back of her neck, along her shoulders, down her arms, but resisted. "We should talk, Danica." Enough of the games. He wanted to tell her everything. He'd just have to deal with the Alicia fallout later. Besides, he was sure he was already in hot water with his sister. She had to have witnessed that kiss. He definitely had some 'plaining to do.

Danica's focus remained on the screen when she said, "I don't want to talk, Weston."

Twenty seconds.

She continued. "I want to live a little. I want to be spontaneous."

Ten seconds.

"I want to..." She paused for a beat. "...make love to you."

Snapsnapsnap.

CHAPTER 6: STAY WITH ME

WESTON WAS SURE THE camera captured the look of delight on his face and hopefully not his surprise. He'd had no expectations for this evening, which made what Danica had just said to him so stunning. Had he even heard her correctly?

Danica shifted and cradled his face between her hands. "Still want to talk?" she asked. "Something tells me no." Her eyes lowered to his crotch, and she smirked.

Yep, he'd heard her correctly.

Hell, no, he didn't want to talk. He wanted to peel her out of that dress and take her right then and there. But as bad as he wanted her, he needed to come clean first. "I'm not who you think I am."

She pulled away, a questioning expression on her face. "Who are you?"

He brushed a bent finger across her cheek. "Will

you allow me to show you?"

When she nodded, he ushered her from the booth, led her out of the ballroom and past the elevator they'd taken earlier. After a maze of turns, they arrived at the private elevator. The lines crawling across Danica's forehead revealed her confusion, but she entered without protest.

Inside the enclosure, they stared at each other, neither breaking the intense silence. He'd give anything to know what was racing through her mind. Would those enticing brown eyes view him differently when she learned the truth? God, he hoped not.

Danica drew in a sharp breath when the elevator came to a halt and the door open. Once they exited, her gaze swooped across every inch of his residence. He followed as she cautiously ambled forward.

"This is who I am," he said.

"I don't…" She turned to face him, the sheer fabric of her dress sweeping the marble floor. "This is the penthouse?"

He folded his arms across his chest and gave a single nod.

She closed the distance between them. "You…live here?"

He nodded again.

"Jesus." She turned and took in more of the space. "Cupid's Arrow must pay very well."

Weston moved close behind her. She flinched when he rested his hands on her waist. He rotated her to face him. "I don't work for Cupid's Arrow; I own it.

Kinda."

"What? Kinda? What...does that mean exactly?"

"It's my sister's company, but I'm a silent partner. Very silent." He laughed, but Danica didn't. "My sister needed my help. Too many women. Not enough men. Long story short, I agreed to be one of her Cupid Fellows for the night." He attempted to interpret the void look on her face, but came up empty. "Say something."

"I..." She rested a hand over her collar bone. "...think I should go," she said, hiking her dress and hurrying toward the elevator.

"Hey," he said, moving after her. "This doesn't change anything. I'm still—"

Danica barked a laugh as she whipped around to face him. "Are you kidding? This changes *everything*."

"How, Danica? I'm the same person I was fifteen minutes ago."

"No, you're not, Weston. Don't you see that?"

"No, I don't. Please, help me understand. Help me *see* it from your perspective." He couldn't believe they were having their first lover's quarrel and weren't even lovers...yet.

Danica placed both hands on either side of her neck and sighed heavily. "Before, you were just a fantasy. Now...you're real. Too real."

"And you prefer living in a fantasy rather than real life?" The words came out harsher than he'd intended.

The level of Danica's voice surprised him when she said, "A fantasy can't hurt you."

Without warning, he claimed her mouth, kissing her with a passion that made him weak. Her delicate hands pushed against his biceps, then cautiously wrapped around them. He clutched her in his arms, digging into the depths of his soul, giving what energy he claimed to her through the kiss.

Danica's body relaxed in his arms. A series of soft moans escaped from them both. To kiss away every ounce of doubt swirling inside of her was his goal. By the way she poured herself into the kiss, he'd accomplished it.

Reluctantly pulling away from her mouth, he stared into her dancing eyes. "Did that hurt?"

In a hushed tone, she said, "No."

"I don't want you to do anything you don't want to do, Danica. I want to make love to you. I want to make love to you so badly, it aches. But the choice is yours."

CHAPTER 7: AS REAL AS IT GETS

ALL OF THE REASONS why Danica shouldn't sleep with Weston blurred the second he'd kissed her inside the ballroom, but now they were back in crystal-clear focus. Fifteen minutes ago, he was Cupid's Fellow, which made him safe, unavailable. Now...he was no longer safe. And *very much* available.

Her thoughts were all over the place. Why did it matter who he was? All she wanted was a night of intense pleasure. No doubt he could give that to her.

That Kiss.

The sensation still lingered on her lips. Her body throbbed, every inch of it. She wanted Weston, needed him, needed this. Needed to feel desired. Making her feel wanted seemed to be a special skill of his.

Why did his identity change anything? So he wasn't who she thought he was. Big deal. They were two consenting adults wanting to spend a night together. Was that so wrong? No.

"Okay," was all she said, all she could manage. Lust held her vocals hostage.

She followed him up the steps to his bedroom like a submissive puppy, the command to stop overridden by her body's selfish need. As they climbed higher and higher, she marveled at her surroundings.

The penthouse rivaled the size of a small country. Warm earth tones gave the massive space a calming vibe. An enormous crystal chandelier dangled above a grand piano positioned by a window that seemed to extend to heaven. Admiring the decorative stair rail, she caught sight of the elevator they'd exited. A freaking elevator. And marble. Marble everywhere.

One thing for sure, Weston Henshaw was loaded. That probably meant he had a different woman in his bed every night. She shook the thought away. He didn't strike her as that kind of guy.

Where in the hell had all of this courage come from? Who was this woman, this bold and daring vixen? Danica didn't know, but she liked her. At least she did tonight. Tomorrow, she'd cast out this reckless persona and revert to the woman who spent Saturday nights on the couch watching reruns of her favorite sitcoms.

Weston's bedroom was as grand as expected. The second they entered, motion-activated lights washed the room in a soft glow, giving it a romantic ambience. The room claimed the same tranquil earth tones and expensive-looking marble. French doors lead to a spacious balcony decorated with black wrought-iron furniture, and a wall of windows gave way to an amazing view of the downtown Raleigh skyline.

"Wow." Sliding her hand from his, she went for a better view. "If I had this view, I'd never get out of bed." Weston stood beside her. "You must—"

He no longer wore the tuxedo jacket and his bowtie dangled around his neck. *Way too sexy*. Her body agreed, sending a booster to her already heightened arousal. His arms were folded across his chest and taut muscles pressed against the fabric of the crisp white shirt he wore.

"—really love this view," she said absently.

His eyes raked over her face, stopping at her lips. The room grew warm as the kiss they'd shared played in her head. But just like that, Weston returned his focus out of the window and so did she.

Danica touched the icy window. "Can they see us?" she asked, referring to the individuals in the neighboring condos.

"No."

Taking a bold move, she positioned her body between him and the glass. She eyed him briefly, unfolded his arms and tugged his shirt from inside his pants.

Weston's arms fell to his sides. He tilted his head and eyed her every move. Once she'd unfastened the last button, she glided her hands up his chiseled torso.

"Take it off," she said, not recognizing the sultry voice that escaped her lips.

He shrugged the shirt off his shoulders, allowing it

55

to fall into a puddle on the floor. Her fingers crawled underneath the white T-shirt he wore, lifting it with every inch dared. Taking the initiative, Weston snatched it over his head. When she ran her hands over his pecs, his nipples hardened.

"You're a beautiful man, Weston Henshaw."

Danica shivered when he pressed her body against the ice-cold window. His masculine scent, his melting warmth aroused her even more. Not wanting to seem overly eager—despite the fact—she resisted the urge to yell, "Take me. Take me now."

Weston lowered his head and kissed her gently, then pulled away. "All night long I've imagined how your lips would feel against mine."

"And how did they feel?"

He gave her another peck. "Like they're where they're meant to be."

She could no longer contribute his words to something he'd been trained to say by Cupid's, because he wasn't truly a Cupid's Fellow. Plus, the words sounded so genuine, so unrehearsed.

He continued. "I've imagined how you would feel wrapped in my arms." As if reading her mind, he said, "Like you belong in them."

A hint of nervousness shook her, but didn't stop her from saying, "Seems we both have active imaginations."

"I want to rip you out of that dress, hoist you into my arms and lose myself deep inside of you."

She reached up to slide the narrow straps off her

shoulders. "What's stopping you?"

Weston captured her hands and lowered them to her sides. "Allow me."

He undressed her in the manner a collector unpacked a priceless doll. When she stood in nothing but red panties and heels, he backed away until he was sitting on the edge of the king-sized bed. "I could sit here and stare at your flawless body all night."

Flawless? Ha. But he thought so, and that was all right with her.

His eyes traveled the length of her body, then back up. "Come here," he said, directing her between his open legs.

Something about Weston conjured her sexy side. Maybe it was the confidence he'd displayed the entire evening. Maybe it was the way he eyed her with admiration. Maybe it was the fact she wanted him like she'd never wanted another man before.

She glided toward him like a runway model. The second she settled in place, he took one of her hardened nipples between his lips and sucked gently. She hummed her delight. Moving to the opposite breast, he circled her nipple with his tongue. Between her legs throbbed, and she wanted Weston to touch her there to relieve the building pressure. "Don't make me wait," she said, her breath catching after the last syllable escaped.

Resting his large hands on her hips, Weston inched her away and stood. He guided her onto the spot he'd occupied and knelt in front of her, kissing her inner thigh. She grew blind with desire.

"You won't need these any more tonight," he said, inching her damp panties from her body. "Did I get you this wet?"

"Yes," she said. "Now what are you going to do about it?"

He chuckled. "I love a challenge."

Seconds later, his warm lips encased her swollen clit and suckled her gently. The move drove a lightning bolt through her entire body, searing her senses. The sensation seized the air in her lungs, and for a moment, she thought she'd blackout. When Weston curved two long fingers inside of her and worked them in just the right spot, her toes curled in her shoes.

Once she'd found her breath again, she repeated, "Yes," over and over.

Weston's technique had her on the verge of an orgasm in record-breaking time. When he softened his tongue and teased her sex bead, she exploded. Her cries cut through the air. Her body quaked under his continued manipulation.

Just when she thought the best of it was over, her body recharged, and she exploded again, sending her back arching completely off the bed. She couldn't translate the words coming out of her own mouth. She was fairly certain they were English...like.

When her body finally stopped shuddering, he removed her heels and guided her to stand. She struggled to maintain her balance, pressing the tips of her fingers into the mattress for added support. Her

legs wobbled and threatened to buckle at any minute.
Sated, she glanced up at the man responsible.
Something glimmered in his eyes and suggested he was
far from done with her.

♡♡♡

Weston dared leaving Danica alone at the foot of
the bed, while he ventured to the nightstand for a
condom. She swayed again, but caught her balance
before toppling over. It'd been a long time since he'd
made a woman that dizzy.

He left a crack in the drawer once he'd removed
the black wrapper. As many times as he intended on
making love to her, opening and closing would only
wear out the rollers.

He stripped off the remainder of his clothing. His
solid erection bounced up and down with each step he
took toward Danica. She appeared enthralled with the
showing. He couldn't read her well enough to know if
she were impressed, startled, or both. The sex gods had
smiled on him, blessing him with length and girth. Not
all women welcomed the combination.

He cradled her face in his hands and captured a
kiss. "Don't worry, I'll be gentle."

A smile twitched at the corners of her mouth and
her drunken eyes danced. "Who's worried?"

Her confidence was an absolute turn on. Weston
kissed her deep and hard while backing her toward the
view she'd been so intrigued with. Placing his hands on

her hips, he rotated her and pinned her flush against the window, lifting her arms above her head and holding them there. She shivered, but didn't complain. The glass frosted from body heat and her labored breathing.

"Are you okay?" he asked.

"P-Perfect."

He planted a tender kiss on the back of her neck, then another on the side. A soft moan floated from her. He nipped her earlobe gently, then kissed it, too. In her ear, he whispered, "Imagine a man craving you so intensely, his every thought, every fantasy has been about you."

"I like the idea," she said in a fragile tone.

Dipping his head, Weston kissed her spine, then trailed kisses all the way to the small of her back. When he cupped her butt cheeks, a delicious sound of delight floated from her. Kissing his way back up, he whispered in her ear again. "I'm that man. I want to make you rethink everything you thought you knew about sex." He rotated her urgently and pinned her back against the frosty glass.

"It's cold," she said, her bottom lip trembling slightly.

Weston tore into the packaging with his teeth, sheathed himself, rested his hands behind her thighs and hoisted her up. "Then I should probably do something about that."

Unhurried, he glided into her warmth. "*Shit*," he said in a throaty tone. He wasn't sure how long he'd be able to last. Being inside of her felt far better than he'd imagined.

Pace yourself.

Danica whimpered each time he entered her with slow, steady strokes. Her body rubbed against the window, producing a sound similar to the one a squeegee made when dragged across a wet glass surface. She sought his mouth, finding him all too willing to give it over to her. Their tongues sparred, teased, delighted in one another's.

Moving away from the window, he never halted his stroke as he carried her to the bed. The plush mattress swallowed them both as they fell into its soft clutch.

The heat generated from their lovemaking intensified her scent. "You taste as delicious as you smell," he said against their joined mouths.

Her hands glided over his sweat-moistened back. Soft cries and the sound of him moving in and out of her wet folds filled the room.

"*Weston...*"

The sound of his name escaping from her was music to his ears...and a caress to his ego. Needing to explore more of her, he positioned a hand behind the bend of her knee, spread her leg further and drove deeper. She cried out, her manicured nails digging into his salty flesh. What should have pained him aroused him instead.

With his mouth inches from hers, he said, "Say my name again." When she did, he captured the last syllable with a greedy kiss.

A beat later, Danica broke away. "I'm..." Her head arched off the pillow. "*Coming*. Don't stop. Please. Don't stop."

She didn't have to worry. The only thing that could stop him was— *Oh, shit*. This. This could stop him. A wave of sensation flooded him, gripping his entire body. She wasn't the only one about to come. *Not now*. He wanted, needed more. *Fight it*.

"Take it, Weston. It's all yours. Give it..."

"You're breaking me, woman. I'm about to shatter." When her muscles clenched around him, milking him, he couldn't hold on any longer. A grunt, then a growl—a sound he couldn't recall ever making— tore through the room. His hips continued to pump until he was sure he'd given her every drop of him. Then he collapsed beside her, pulling her shuddering body into his arms.

"That was..." She paused. "You were..." She paused again. "I need a nap."

"I'll take that as a compliment." He kissed the top of her head.

Her chest heaved up and down. "You definitely should."

Weston draped the comforter over them and held Danica's bare body as if she'd dart from his bed if he loosened his grip. She didn't seem to mind, snuggling her head in the crook of his neck.

Their bodies were positioned in a manner that allowed them to take full advantage of the spectacular view outside. The night was so clear it resembled a painting with a thousand stars twinkling in the midnight sky. From now on, when he lie in bed admiring the sight, he'd have this moment to remember.

"Did you see that?" Danica asked.

"See what?"

"A shooting star."

"No, I missed it." He kissed her shoulder. "Did you make a wish?"

"Of course I did."

He tightened his arms around her. "You think it'll come true?" He'd never been one for wishing upon a star.

"It just did. I wished you'd hold me tighter."

The words only amplified what he was feeling. What was it about this woman that made him *wish* the night would never end? "You didn't need a star to make that happen. I'd gladly hold you as tight and as long as you'd like."

"Really?" she said, amusement present in her tone. "So, if I wanted you to hold me for the next forty-eight hours, you would?"

"Without question or letting go."

She laughed. "And what if you had to su-su?"

"Had to...what?" he asked with laughter in his voice.

"It's something my grandmother used to say. I spent most summers with her in Florida. Every Sunday before we left for church, she'd ask me if I had to su-su. *Pee*. The term sorta stuck with me."

"*Ahhh*. Okay. Now it makes sense, I guess."

"Hey, don't be making fun of my grandmother." She pinched his nipple playfully.

"Ouch." He captured her fingers and kissed each one. "Well, if I had to *su-su*, I'd just wrap you in my arms likes this..." He did a swift motion that ended with her on his chest. "...and take you with me."

Danica giggled like an overjoyed child. The sound made him smile. He delighted in being the one making her laugh. He got the impression she'd known a lot of pain in her past. She settled and he encased her in his arms again.

"Weston?"

Uh-oh. This wasn't the sensual way she'd called his name earlier. "Yes?"

"Why share with me who you really are?"

"It seemed like the right thing to do."

"Oh."

Had he just given the wrong answer?

"Do you always do what's right?"

"Yes. At least, I try."

Tonight would fall into the try category. He'd tried to convince himself that Danica was only business. It hadn't worked. He'd tried to resist her. That hadn't worked either. Yep, tonight...he'd fallen short on doing the right thing.

Right would have been to not have touched her. Right would have been to not have kissed her. Right would have been to not have tasted her, made love to her, fallen for her. Sometimes, right yielded to wrong.

A beat of silence fell between them. He couldn't help but wonder what was racing through her mind.

"What about work?" she continued. "If you're keeping me captive in your arms, how would you work?"

"My staff is extremely capable. They run this place without me pretty much every day."

Danica's head rose. "This place?"

Just another minute fact he'd omitted. "I own De Lore." He studied the quizzical expression on her face. Was that a good or bad thing?

"Bachelors in Business Magazine."

Jesus. After a year, that article still haunted him. He knew exactly where this conversation was headed. "What about it?"

"That's why you looked so familiar to me." She smoothed her hand over his cheek. "You didn't have a beard in the photo, though."

"Alicia convinced me to get rid of it for the photo shoot."

"I like the beard. It makes you look...distinguished."

"I'm glad I have your approval."

Danica tucked her hand back into the crook of his neck. "It was an interesting article."

Weston groaned when he recalled agreeing to the article. That editorial had made him sound like the biggest player in North Carolina. They'd glazed over mention of the numerous charities he was involved with, his work with Habitat for Humanity, even his own foundation that helped ex-convicts transition back into society. They had, however, highlighted all of his rumored escapades with models, actresses, and socialites. He was sure *that* was the part Danica found interesting.

"I'm not that guy," he said in an attempt to stave off any misconceptions.

"You didn't buy your first property when you were twenty-one? Make your first million at twenty-five? Name De Lore after your deceased mother?"

Wow. She had read the article. "Yes, but—"

"But you're referring to the two full pages detailing your *active* social life, right?"

"Yes. That article was a PR nightmare. Not to mention, extremely embellished."

"Hmm. I don't know. The part about you having women clamoring for your attention was awfully convincing."

"What did you do, commit the article to memory?" he asked, pinching her butt.

Danica squealed and nibbled his neck playfully. "No. The article inspired me. You inspired me. The things you'd accomplished, and at such a young age. I didn't pay much attention to the other stuff. I mean, who could fault you? You're not married, not in a relationship. You should be having single-man fun."

Weston trailed his fingers up and down Danica's arm. "Yeah, I guess."

If she thought tonight was about him having *single-man fun*, he could assure her, it had become about far more.

CHAPTER 8: ONCE THE FOG CLEARS

WHEN DANICA OPENED HER eyes, she still lolled in the same spot she'd fallen asleep—Weston's arms. His chest moved up and down and her body rose and fell with it. He snored. Just a little. Even fast asleep, he was a striking man.

Why was she still here with him? She'd gotten what she wanted—needed. A night filled with unparalleled passion. She'd ordered; he'd delivered. The things he'd done to her body...unforgettable. Her assumption had been accurate. He was a dynamic lover.

Her swollen bladder suggested her need to find the bathroom. All she had to do was figure out which of the four doors led there. She kissed her index and middle fingers and pressed them gently to Weston's lips before inching out of his arms. She paused when his snoring ceased. When it started again, she eased out of the bed.

The open drawer caught Danica's eye. Something—call it curiosity, or by its less flattering name, nosiness—forced her to inch the drawer open further.

Oh. Wow.

Condoms. Not a box or two. More like a case, several cases even, packed the drawer. It brought her back to a dreadful place. A place where she'd opened her ex-husband's glove box and a half used box of condoms fell out—the exact brand as she stared at now. Was this fate playing a cruel joke on her?

Danica glanced at Weston and an image of her ex-husband flashed in her head. She saw the lipstick on the collar, smelled the scent of a fragrance she'd never worn. Remembered the agony and pain of long, lonesome nights. Relived every lie he'd told her over the course of their marriage. It all came rushing back.

Her chest tightened, and it became hard to breath. Instincts shot red flags into the air, all directing her to the nearest exit. The Bachelors in Business article popped into her head. Three words in particular: A POWERFUL MAN. That's how Weston had been described.

One thing she'd learned from her philandering ex about powerful men—one of anything was never enough for them. Including women.

The connection and chemistry she'd experienced all night with Weston beckoned her to stay. History and the fear of knowing she wanted more than just casual sex summoned her to leave. Something about him clouded her judgment. Deciphering right from wrong proved difficult when it came to him. She needed to escape before she fell further than she already had. Plus, it was easier this way. Their saying goodbye was inevitable. No use delaying it.

The fantasy was fun while it lasted.

With that thought, she gathered her clothes and tip-toed toward the bedroom door.

♡♡♡

Weston had always been a light sleeper, so he knew the second Danica fled his arms and his bed. He also knew she'd seen the overkill of condoms in his drawer. He could only imagine what sordid thoughts about him raced through her mind.

The condoms were easily explained. When you owned a company that produced condoms, you got condoms. Plenty of them. What she couldn't know was that he hadn't removed a single one from the drawer in over eight months.

The condoms weren't the only thing that had her spooked. Couldn't have been. Not by the determined manner in which she moved about the room. He remained silent, watching with partially open eyes in hopes that she would abandon the notion of leaving and climb back into his arms. When she neared the door, he knew that wasn't going to happen.

"Hey?" He came up on his elbows.

Danica's body jerked like a thief who'd been

caught making off with diamonds and pearls. "Hey," she said, making a cautious rotation toward him.

"Where are you going?"

"I... I was..."

"Were you sneaking out?" No doubt her escape had played out much better in her head.

A nervous laugh escaped. "No. I wasn't *sneaking* out. I was simply leaving. You were sleeping so peacefully, and I didn't want to wake you."

He rested his elbows on his bent knees, clasped his fingers together and stared at her. It was all he could do to keep his eyes from trailing over her exposed parts. Regaining focus, he forced a smile to hide his irritation. "That was very thoughtful of you."

"I had a great time last evening, Weston. We don't have to pretend this is more than what it is. You got what you wanted. I got what I needed. I don't regret spending the night with you. It was amazing. I hope you don't regret it."

She made their night together sound like some meaningless tryst. But how in the hell could he argue with her with such a vulnerable expression on her face? "I don't." Inwardly, he wanted her to stay, but if she wanted to leave, he wouldn't try to stop her. Despite how desperately he wanted to.

"Good."

What did he say next? Have a great life? See you around?

After a couple more seconds of grueling silence, she said, "I should go." She moved away again.

He sighed, bringing forth a fact she clearly hadn't considered. "How are you getting home, Danica? You didn't drive here, remember?"

"I'm sure I can get a cab."

Or maybe she had considered it. "Let me get dressed. I'll drive you home."

"You don't—"

"I insist." He gave her a *there's no need to argue* glance. She obviously interpreted it because she didn't utter another word.

Out of the bed, he sighed to himself. Was this it? They'd spent an amazing evening together—her words, but he completely agreed—and this was how they were going to end things? With an "I had a great time."

Damn.

Weston excused himself to the bathroom. Staring at his reflection in the mirror, he shook his head. This wasn't how their time together was supposed to conclude. Not with him making love to her only once. Passion this intense was supposed to spill into the wee hours of the morning. They would capture a few hours of sleep, then start all over again with their lovemaking pouring into the following evening.

Clearly, Danica hadn't had the same thoughts. After su-suing, he brushed his teeth and washed his face. "If that's how she wants it, that's how it'll be." That ridiculous notion only lasted a second. He wanted her in his life and had roughly a thirty minute car ride to figure out exactly what to say to make it happen.

On second thought, he knew exactly what to say.

He rushed from the bathroom like a man full of fight. When he reentered the bedroom, it was empty. A second later, the sound of the elevator chiming drew him from the room.

Weston reached the top of the staircase just as the doors were closing. Their eyes held a split second, then she was gone.

CHAPTER 9: BE MINE

WESTON RESTED HIS HEAD against his leather office chair, staring at the ceiling. There were a million things he should have been accomplishing, but none of them compelled him enough to pull his thoughts away from Danica James.

He'd given her ten long days...Ten. Long. Days, to discover how right they were for each other. Nothing. Not a phone call, text, or email. But what did he actually expect from the woman who'd sneaked out while he was in the bathroom?

Sure, he could have easily picked up the phone and called her. But she'd been the one to run away from him, not the other way around. He wanted to be angry at her, but honestly, he couldn't. She'd run for a reason. He wanted to believe it wasn't to simply get away from him.

Maybe it was to get away from what was swirling

between them. Hell, he felt it. The moment he'd laid eyes on her, he felt it. She had to feel it, too. The attraction. The pull. The chemistry. Chemistry that ranked off the charts.

The door creaked behind him, drawing him from his thoughts.

"You should be doing a happy dance around your office since that fraudulent lawsuit was dropped. But here you are, staring at the ceiling...again. What is eating at you, Bizzy? These past couple of days, you've seemed stressed. Weston Henshaw doesn't do stressed, remember?"

Alicia. This was so not a good time.

Not only did The Henshaw Towers house his company, The Henshaw Group, it was also home to Cupid's Arrow. Which meant his sister could pop in anytime she wanted. Not an issue most days, but today, he needed to be alone with his thoughts.

This situation with Danica had him off his game. He couldn't shake her from his system as easily as she'd seemingly shaken him. She lingered. Always there. In his thoughts, his dreams.

He'd never been one to assign blame to anyone, but in this case... "This is entirely your fault," he said, turning to face Alicia. "I never should have agreed to be one of your Cupid gigolos."

"I'm offended. Cupid's Arrow does not employ *gigolos*. And what's entirely my fault? What happened?" she asked, sitting on the edge of his desk.

Alicia had no idea what'd happened between him

and Danica on Valentine's—other than the kiss in the ballroom—but he'd explained that away. Today, he wasn't in any mood to be chewed out by her for sleeping with a client. He returned to a reclined position and waved his words off. "Nothing." But he'd already said too much.

A slow, wide grin lit her face. "I don't believe it. I truly don't believe it. That kiss did more than make Calvin Fairchild green-eyed. You fell for her. You fell for the sexy vixen in red. I mean, I see how; she's gorgeous. I've had five of my male clients inquire about her."

The idea of Danica giving her time to any other man agitated him. He massaged away an impending headache.

"Weston Henshaw doesn't fall. Nor does he mix business with pleasure. What in the hell kind of voodoo did she work on you?" Alicia asked.

The kind that had him up most nights thinking about her. He'd broken two of his cardinal rules. Never show vulnerability, and never mix business with pleasure. He and Danica had done a whole lotta mixing. He laughed out loud, not believing what he'd gotten himself into.

"What's funny?"

Weston ignored the question. "I told her about Dad's accident." His eyes held Alicia's.

Her expression turned severe. She eased off his desk and into the chair across from him.

"Wow. This is serious. You rarely talk to *me* about Dad's accident. You really like this woman, huh?"

He jolted forward, rested his forearms on the desk and intertwined his fingers. Lowering his gaze, he recalled how Danica had comforted him while he told her one of the most painful stories of his life. The concern she'd shown—genuine concern—touched him. "I can't explain it, but yeah, I do. I'm crazy about her."

Whether or not Danica chose to admit it, they'd connected on a level far beyond just sexual. Whatever had caused her to run had something to do with her ex-husband. He could feel it. Alicia cut into his thoughts with one simple question.

"What are you going to do?"

"Nothing," danced on the tip of his tongue, but that would have been a lie.

♡♡♡

Danica's index finger hovered above the enter key for the tenth time in just as many days. Googling Weston made her feel stalker-ish, but she desperately needed to steal a glimpse of him. Even if it were only via a computer monitor. All she had to do was hit enter, and she'd have her fix.

"Danica?"

Danica flinched at the sound of her assistant's voice. "Yes, Lizzy?"

"I'm going to take my lunch now, if that's okay?"

"Yes. That's fine." Danica cleared Weston's name from the search box, then stood from behind her desk. "On second thought, why don't you take the remainder of the afternoon off? I can handle things here."

Lizzy's brows arched, flashing her surprise. Rarely did Danica close the office early, but with the threat of winter weather, she figured it best Lizzy got a head start on the gridlock that occurred in North Carolina with the simple hint of bad weather.

"Are you sure?"

Danica smiled and shooed the woman out. "Yes, go on. I promise I won't mangle things too severely. I'm headed out in a few myself. I think we actually might get snow this time."

Lizzy seemed to consider the offer for a moment, then shrugged. "I guess I should swing by the grocery store for milk and bread," she said.

"You don't drink milk," Danica said.

"I know, but isn't that what you North Carolinians do at the first mention of a snowflake?"

Both women laughed.

"Drive safely," Danica said.

"You, too," said Lizzy, exiting the office.

Once Lizzy was out of sight, Danica walked to her fourth floor office window and stared at the world below. People and cars bustled by. The sky donned a grayish-blue hue. The scene was soothing, but the view in no way compared to the one from Weston's penthouse.

Weston.

She'd spent just one night with him. How could she still long for him close to two weeks later? Was it because he'd taken her body to extreme sexual peaks?

Or was it something more? It pained her to cop to the latter. Truth was, Weston Henshaw had touched her in a way that she didn't believe possible. In such a short span of time, he'd touched her heart. And she'd walked away with not so much as a goodbye. Fear made you do stupid things.

"Dammit."

This is what she'd dreaded most. Missing him. And every day that sailed past, she missed him a little more. Missed his touch. Missed his kisses. Missed his presence. How long would she ache for him?

All she had to do was pick up the phone and call him. Yeah, right. She didn't even have the courage to hit enter on the damn keyboard. Besides, she was probably the last person he wanted to hear from. Something inside of her had hoped he'd reach out to her. He hadn't, and she understood why. At least, had convinced herself she understood.

Remembering the conversation she'd had with Savannah earlier, she blew out a long, heated breath that frosted the window. With her index finger, she drew a heart with an arrow through it. *Cupid's Arrow*.

When Savannah had asked if she thought about Weston, she'd lied. No way could she cop to him saturating her thoughts. Not only did she think about him. She dreamed about him. Dreamed about him every single night. Daydreamed about him every single day. Why in the hell was he so hard to forget? It wasn't like they'd spent years together, though it felt like they had.

All she'd ever wanted, ever needed was for someone to make her feel the way Weston had in just one night. Was she really supposed to simply forget? She closed her eyes and shook her head. Of course she was. She had to. For her own sanity, if for nothing else.

"We never should have happened. Cupid's made an error. We were never supposed to meet."

Danica's body stiffened as the velvety tone caressed her entire body. Funny how certain sounds triggered amazing memories. Taking a deep breath and releasing it slowly, she rotated to face him. "Weston?"

Sweet baby Jesus.

Her eyes soaked up every inch of him. From the black skull cap toboggan to the black button-neck cable sweater. A charcoal-colored scarf draped his neck. The high-collar coat he wore claimed the same shade of gray as the scarf. Dark denim jeans over black boots completed the ensemble. The outfit probably cost a fortune. The way he wore the garments...priceless.

Her heart rapped against her ribcage. Gathering her thoughts, she said, "What are you talking about?"

"You were supposed to be some woman named Grace, who loved Brussels sprouts, disliked most outdoor activities, and was allergic to chocolate."

"I hate Brussels sprouts," she said, folding her arms across her chest. "W-What are you doing here, Weston?" Not that she wasn't happy to see him.

He neared, removing the expensive-looking black leather gloves. A twinge of nervousness rattled her. It had to be from the look in those powerful brown eyes.

She smoothed a hand over the fabric of her long-sleeved, onyx-colored dress. Suddenly, she felt unstable in the black, knee-high, heeled boots.

"I'm here for you," he said plain and simple.

His stone-faced expression alerted her to the gravity of his words. "Here for..." She swallowed hard, but it wasn't enough to loosen the painful lump in her throat. "...me?" she croaked out.

"I've tried to forget you. Not because I wanted to, but because I needed to. You're lousy for business." He flashed a brilliant smile. "I can't focus on anything but the thought of you, Danica. I've never experienced this before."

"Ex—" Her words stuck again. Trying a second time, she said, "Experienced what?"

"Wanting a woman the way I want you. Needing a woman the way I need you."

She swayed and Weston reached out to steady her. "I'm okay," she said, pushing his hands from her hips and taking a step or two back. She couldn't think straight with him standing so close, let alone touching her. "What makes you think you want or need me? You don't even know me."

"I know you're the most sincere and compassionate woman I've met in a long time. I'm drawn to you like a magnet. When it comes to you, Danica James, I don't think. I feel. This *feels* right. *We* feel right. There's a reason I ended up on your doorstep Valentine's Day."

Yes, this did feel right. So right. And she wanted to

scream it at the top of her lungs. But she needed to approach this with caution. She'd given into what her heart wanted once. She'd gotten hurt—crushed. "I don't know…" At a loss for words, she folded her arms across her chest again and eyed him.

"I want you in my life. I need you in my life. What I feel for you shouldn't be this strong. Not after just one night. I know this seems irrational, but…" He shrugged. "I'm crazy about you, woman."

"I walked away from you," she said.

"Yes, you did. I know you had your reasons. What are they? Was it the condoms in the drawer?"

Danica rested her hand on the side of her neck. "Amid other things."

"Like…what?" When she didn't readily answer, he said, "Your ex-husband?"

She nodded. "I went through a lot with him. I gave him all of me, and it wasn't enough. If I wasn't enough for him, how could I ever be enough for a man like you?"

Weston's brows crumpled. "A man like me? Who am I, Danica?"

"You're a mogul who can have any woman on any continent he wants."

"You have me all wrong. I'm just a man who is crazy about one woman, on this continent. That woman is you. You shouldn't question if you're enough for me. I should question if I'm enough for you. You're a treasure, Danica James. I knew it after only one hour with you. Your ex-husband was a damn fool to sacrifice a pot of gold."

Danica swallowed hard in an attempt to push back her emotions. "Th-Thank you for saying that."

Weston glanced to his left. "Is this the desk your mother purchased for you? The one that's so dear to your heart?"

She nodded, not sure where this conversation was headed.

He walked parallel to the desk, gliding his fingers over the glass top. "This desk gave you the courage to start something new. Gave you the strength you needed to take that first step toward your dream." He stilled, his back to her. "I want to offer you something that will give you the courage to take an even bigger leap of faith. Offer you something that will give you the strength to forget the hurt you've experienced in your past."

"Yeah? And what is that?"

He turned to face her. "My heart." He neared her slowly. "I'm offering you every beat of my heart."

In a voice saturated with emotion, she said, "I'm scared, Weston." The admission made her vulnerable, but somehow, she knew he wouldn't take advantage.

"Maybe what scares you is the fact that you want and need me, too." He removed the scarf he wore, held it in two hands and lassoed her with it. Pulling her to him, he said, "You don't have to fear falling in love with me."

Love?

Another wave of uneasiness whizzed through her.

Had he fallen in love with her? Had she fallen in love with him? Is that why she'd been unable to simply let him go? Was love after one night even possible?

The scent of his cologne acted as a pleasure trigger, soothing her frayed nerves.

Weston held her flush to his chest and tilted her chin with his index finger. "I didn't intend on falling for you, but I did. You talk about being scared? What I feel for you scares the hell out of me. I've been down this road before, and I got crushed. The fact that I'm willing to sacrifice my heart again lets me know…" He paused, his lips partially open.

"Let's you know what?"

"That you're the one, Danica. It lets me know that you're the one. I want you to be my forever Valentine. I want to be your forever Cupid's Fellow."

"*Oh*," she said, attempting to process it all.

"And about the condoms in my drawer… I own the company that produces them. They've been there—untouched—for close to a year."

Owned a condom company? How many ventures did this man have?

"Danica, I know you've been hurt in the past. I know your heart has been broken, but give me the opportunity to show you how you should be loved."

As hard as she fought it, a tear trickled from her eye. Did she fight or follow her heart? "I haven't stopped thinking about you from the moment I walked away. I do feel something for you, Weston. Something powerful. But how do we know? How do we know that what we're feeling is real? It was just one *amazing, unforgettable, earth-shattering* night."

They shared a much needed laugh.

"Seriously, Weston. Are these types of feelings born in *one* night?" She shrugged. "How do we know?"

Weston echoed her words. "How do we know?"

He held her face between his hands and kissed her tearstained cheek. A beat later, he captured her mouth and ravished it with an energy that had to come from the depths of his soul. If the effects his kisses had on her body were any indication, maybe they were meant to be.

A heated sensation crawled up her spine, warmed her neck and spread to every other part of her body. She wanted him right then and there. When Weston broke away from her mouth, she searched feverishly for more of him.

"Open your eyes," he said.

She compiled, feeling a gush of euphoria seeing him.

"Did that feel real?" he asked.

Her eyes slid away. "Yes, but..." Her words trailed off.

"Look at me, Danica."

She did.

"Yes, but what?"

But what if it doesn't—? She stopped the thought dead in its tracks. *What if it does?*

Danica stared into Weston's eyes, into his soul. What she observed squashed all doubt she held. If this was a mistake, it was a mistake worth making. With a full heart and a bright smile, she said, "But you have to promise to never stop kissing me like you can't get enough of me."

"*Oh*, I think I can manage that. Besides, I *can't* get enough of you." He nestled her into his arms. "I'm looking forward to falling in love with you, Danica James."

"I'm looking forward to falling in love with you, Weston Henshaw." Though, she was pretty sure she was already there. "Remind me to contact your sister later."

Weston reared back to look at her. "My sister? Dare I ask why?"

Danica smirked. "I need to thank her for Cupid's error."

THE END

ABOUT THE AUTHOR

Joy Avery is a North Carolina native with a passion for penning contemporary romances. Her stories guide readers along the rutted roads of love, delivering them to a gratifying happily ever after.

Joy is a member of Romance Writers of America and Heart of Carolina Romance Writers.

When she's not writing, she enjoys reading, cake decorating, pretending to expertly play the piano, driving her husband insane, and playing with her sixteen-pound peek-a-poo and hundred-pound Rottweiler.

Also by Joy Avery

Smoke in the Citi
His Until Sunrise-an Indigo Falls romance

Dear Reader,

I hope you've enjoyed reading **CUPID'S ERROR**. Please help me spread the word about Danica and Weston by recommending their love story to friends and family, book clubs, and online forums.

Also, please take a moment to leave a review on the site where you purchased this novel.

I love hearing from readers. Feel free to email me at: authorjoyavery@gmail.com.

WHERE YOU CAN FIND ME:

WWW.JOYAVERY.COM

FACEBOOK.COM/AUTHORJOYAVERY

TWITTER.COM/AUTHORJOYAVERY

PINTEREST.COM/AUTHORJOYAVERY

AUTHORJOYAVERY@GMAIL.COM

Please visit my website to sign up for my "WINGS OF LOVE" newsletter and get updates on new releases, special offers, bonus content, giveaways, and contests:

Made in the USA
Charleston, SC
12 March 2015

ML   5-15